CHARMSEEKERS: BOOK TWO

The Silver Pool

Georgie Adams

Illustrated by Gwen Millward

Orion
Children's Books

First published in Great Britain in 2008
by Orion Children's Books
Reissued 2011 by Orion Children's Books
a division of the Orion Publishing Group Ltd
Orion House
5 Upper St Martin's Lane
London WC2H 9EA
An Hachette UK Company

3 5 7 9 8 6 4 2

ISBN 978 1 4440 0290 4

Printed and bound by CPI Group (UK) Ltd, Croydon, CR0 4YY

www.orionbooks.co.uk

For my parents –
Douglas and Georgina
With love and gratitude
Amy

The Thirteen Charms of Karisma

When Charm became queen of Karisma, the wise
and beautiful Silversmith made her a precious gift.
It was a bracelet. On it were fastened thirteen
silver amulets, which the Silversmith called
"charms", in honour of the new queen.

It was part of Karisma law. Whenever there was
a new ruler the Silversmith made a special gift, to
help them care for the world they had inherited.
And this time it was a bracelet. She told Queen
Charm it was magical because the charms held
the power to control the forces of nature and
keep everything in balance. She must take the
greatest care of them. As long as she, and she
alone, had possession of the charms all would
be well.

And so it was, until the bracelet was stolen by
the spider, and fell into the hands of Zorgan, the
magician. Then there was chaos!

In the soft glow of candlelight the Silversmith sits and reflects. Her Charmseeker's quest has begun. Sesame has found the bracelet and heart charm, and has taken them to the Outworld for safekeeping.

One of the thirteen magic candles has gone out. Twelve lighted candles remain and each will burn until its charm has been found. Will Sesame find the courage to see her mission through?

"I have chosen well," says the Silversmith, confident she has made the right decision about Sesame Brown. "She will return to continue her quest, of that I have no doubt!"

One

Zorgan paced the floor, his thoughts swirling like a whirlpool, as he dwelt on some recent, unfortunate events. His plan to take possession of the bracelet had gone badly wrong – his old adversary the Silversmith had seen to that! At the very thought of her, fury welled up inside him. He was convinced she had put a spell on the bracelet to prevent him, or anyone but Queen Charm, from wearing it – the black mark on his wrist was a constant and painful reminder that it had done its job.

The sorcerer recalled the fleeting sensation of joy he'd experienced when he'd put the bracelet on. Oh! The power that should have been his! But no, it was not to be. Angrily, Zorgan banged his fist on a table, cursing himself for scattering the charms. Now he must find and destroy them. The race was on to get them back!

The *bang* startled three companions who were with Zorgan in his study. The bandrall, Vanda, perched on a high-backed chair and the pixie puppets, Nix and Dina.

"Two new creations of my own," Zorgan had told Vanda, when introducing the pixies for the first time. To the casual observer Nix and Dina looked like normal pixie girls, with their flowing hair and impish faces. But closer inspection would reveal cold crystal eyes and steely wings, fine as cobweb; the pixies could fly like deadly arrows and were programmed to obey Zorgan without question.

The sudden noise unsettled Vanda.

"Rashee,rashee," * cooed Zorgan soothingly,

* *

Rashee – hush; be still; a word of reassurance

4

stroking her neck. Ever since Vanda had come to roost on Zorgan's Tower, he'd taken an instant liking to her. The two had become inseparable. She flapped her wings to steady herself, before settling again on the chair.

Vanda watched as Zorgan turned to Nix and Dina. They stood alert, awaiting orders.

"The time has come to try you out," said Zorgan. "Set you tasks. Test your skills."

Nix and Dina's sharp eyes glinted in anticipation.

"You remember that, er, unfortunate incident with the charm bracelet?" he said, admiring a large gaudy ring on his finger.

Zorgan paused, waiting to see if Nix and Dina understood. They responded immediately.

"Yes, Master!" they chorused.

"When you put the bracelet on, it burned you," said Nix.

"So you threw it away!" added Dina enthusiastically.

"Spallah!"* exclaimed Zorgan, delighted with their response. "Well, I must get those charms back and destroy them. But there are those who wish to keep them. They must be stopped!"

"Who?" asked Dina.

"Morbrecia, for a start," he replied. "Queen Charm's sister. She's determined to find them, foolish girl,

* *

*✶ **Spallah** – excellent!; a triumphant expression

though I doubt they'll do her any good. Besides, she's mad at me!"

Dina remembered Zorgan had tricked Morbrecia into stealing the bracelet from the queen. She'd been furious when Zorgan threw it away.

"Orders understood!" said Dina, with a malicious grin.

"Good," said Zorgan.

"Who else?" asked Nix, eager to prove herself too.

Zorgan hesitated. He wasn't sure, but he'd heard stories about an Outworlder. A girl called Sesame . . . Sesame . . . *Brown*! She'd been seen near Charm's palace.

"There's a girl . . ." he said, his voice cold as ice. "An interfering Outworlder. She'll be sorry she ever set foot in Karisma. I want to know all about Sesame Brown!"

The pixies shuddered at the venom in his voice.

"It shall be done, Master!" said Nix and Dina.

And in a whirr of wings they were off.

6

Zorgan's study was circular, as were all the others in the tower, tiered like the layers of a cake. It was lined from floor to ceiling with bookshelves, perfectly curved to fit the walls. The sorcerer's library contained hundreds of books on Astronomy, Astrology, Folklore, Myth and Magic.

After Nix and Dina had gone, he crossed the room to select some books from the shelves. Vanda followed, alighting on a chandelier, the better to observe Zorgan from her lofty perch. She watched him now scanning a row of leather-bound volumes.

First Zorgan took down *A Discourse with Dragons*

by Perdika Klum. The author, a famous dracomologist, had spent a lifetime studying dragons and had learned to speak their language – Dracodictum. There was a list of phrases in her book that he would find useful. Next he selected *A Pool of Silver* and, after a quick look along a row of encyclopedias, he found an old copy of *Rare Chants and Incantations*.

"Ah, yes," said Zorgan, blowing a layer of dust from the cover. "I'll need that too."

Clasping the weighty tomes to his chest, Zorgan staggered up the spiral staircase to his Star Room – exactly one hundred and ninety-five twisty steps to the top of the tower. Vanda flew ahead, screeching with delight, in her element to be flying higher and higher.

The Star Room was entirely encased in glass. Zorgan stood for a moment to catch his breath, and take in the view of the heavens. It was magnificent! The sheer vastness of the starry night sky never failed to enthral. Up here the sorcerer felt exhilarated. Here he could do magic!

Looking out across Karisma, Zorgan fixed his gaze on Mount Fortuna in the distance. In no time he had conjured a vision of the Silver Pool, and the Silversmith who had charge of it. He would soon have his revenge on her!

But to achieve that, he had work to do. Seating himself comfortably in an armchair, he opened *A Pool of Silver* and started to read . . .

A Pool of Silver
by the Silversmith

PUBLISHED BY FORTUNA BOOKS, KARISMA

Introduction by the Silversmith

The liquid silver, found in a pool on Mount Fortuna, is unique to Karisma and quite unlike the precious metal of other worlds. The exact origin of the Silver Pool is unknown although one thing is certain; the pool has existed for as long as anyone can remember, because no matter how much silver is used the pool always refills itself — like magic!

Various stories have been told which attempt to explain how it may have come about but the most popular belief, held by Karismans today, is based on this intriguing legend.

The Legend of the Silver Pool

In far off days, when dragons were as common as cats, a huge dragon called Agapogo* lived in a cave on Mount Fortuna, guarding a vast hoard of silver. A glittering pile of coins, candlesticks, dishes, plates, trays, jewellery and ornaments were piled high from floor to ceiling.

How Agapogo came by this amazing treasure or what she intended to do with it remains a mystery, but she defended the silver as if her life depended upon it. And, for a hundred years or more, no one dared come near. The sound of her roaring rumbled like thunder. People got so used to the noise, they took no notice. Until the day it stopped.

* *

* **Agapogo** – a favourite name for dragons, means "to spit fire"

10

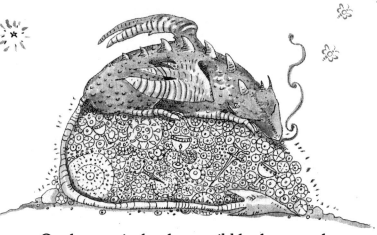

On that particular day a gribbler happened
to be walking on the mountain and fell into
the cave. When he recovered from his fall,
the gribbler couldn't believe his luck. Here
was a cave full of treasure and Agapogo
sound asleep! He was sure he could steal
some things and be off, before she woke up.
Which might have worked, if the gribbler
hadn't made a silly mistake. Because out of
that enormous hoard he couldn't resist a fine
silver goblet,* right under her nose!

* *

*Goblet – a goblet, reputed to be the one stolen
from Agapogo, is used by gribblers today in
ceremonies, in which a powerful potion of leaves
is sipped from the cup

Now a wiser thief might have thought twice about taking it, but not this one — it's well known that gribblers are not very bright. As soon as Agapogo felt the goblet move she opened her eyes and, seeing the gribbler standing there with her treasure, she got red-hot flaming mad! She swung her tail like a boolly* bat (a sure sign a dragon is really upset) sending everything flying. She roared SO loudly the mountain shook and flames burst from her nostrils like twin volcanoes.

And here is the most remarkable part of the story; the heat from those two blazing jets MELTED all the silver! Everything in that pile of treasure, down to the last tiny teaspoon,

* *

*Boolly – a traditional Karisman ball game, played with a boolly bat and ball

dissolved like butter. It made a pool of silver
SO deep that Agapogo drowned.

How the gribbler survived Agapogo's flames
and lashing tail, we shall never know. But he
did and was the only one to witness the last
few moments of the dragon's life. The gribbler
is reputed to have told a friend :

"Agapogo tried to save herself, thrashing and
writhing about, something awful. Then she
gurgled and sank to the bottom and some big
bubbles came popping up."

A thin smile crept across Zorgan's lips as he closed the book.

"An unfortunate end for Agapogo," he told Vanda, at the same time reaching for *A Discourse with Dragons*. Then, having checked the pronunciation of some words in Dracodictum, Zorgan stood up and opened his copy of *Rare Chants and Incantations* at a page he had previously marked. Silently he mouthed the words. His hands shook. Zorgan was a powerful magician but he knew the risks. If he made a mistake, said one wrong word . . . there was no knowing what might happen! He took a deep breath and intoned:

★ APOST
      SNARGAL
           INCENDUS ★
               AGAPOGO!

A terrifying wind howled around the tower, and a blast of freezing air hit him full in the face. Then a ghostly dragon appeared, spinning out of nowhere like a tornado, its massive wings spread like sails. Silvery scales glowed eerily in the dark and in its scythe-like talons the phantom gripped a goblet. Zorgan had summoned the spirit of Agapogo – the dragon of the Silver Pool!

The force of the blast threw Zorgan to the floor. Vanda flew round the room in a panic, screeching in terror. Slowly picking himself up, Zorgan bowed and addressed Agapogo in Dracodictum:

★ "Drink the pool of silver dry,
Or in its depths forever lie.
★ I command you to obey;
Drain every drop without delay!" ★

A streak of lightning slashed the night sky, followed by an ear-splitting *crack* of thunder.

Then the spirit of Agapogo spoke, every word a blast of fury:

"You dare to call me from the deep
And wake me from eternal sleep?
Magician, you are a fool
To bid me drink the precious pool!
I'd fight this spell, if I were free,
Alas, this wicked plan must be.
It shall be done but you shall see,
Revenge shall be my guarantee!"

There was a blinding flash of light and a tremendous explosion. Instinctively Zorgan cowered and hid his face. When he looked again Agapogo's spirit had vanished in a cloud of smoke, leaving the sound of the spirit's words ringing in his ears.

Two

It was a hot Friday afternoon, the last day of school before half-term. Sesame Brown sat in class, doodling in her notebook. Her best friend, Maddy Webb, was sitting next to her watching her doodle. Neither was concentrating much on what their history teacher, Mrs Wilks, was saying.

One reason was because Sesame and Maddy had just started riding lessons. Their riding instructor Miss Luck had suggested they come and help at the stables during half-term.

"You'll learn a lot about ponies that way," she'd said.

But there was another reason. Ever since her adventure in Karisma, Sesame kept thinking about what had happened there.

Mrs Wilks turned away to type something into her computer, and Maddy passed Sesame a note:

What's that?

"Something I found," whispered Sesame. "When I went to . . ."

She stopped. Mrs Wilks had turned round and was looking straight at her!

"Who can tell me the name of the city?" she asked, pointing to an image she had just downloaded onto the white board. "Sesame. How about you?"

Sesame's class had been learning about the Romans, and Mrs Wilks had been telling them about a volcano, which had erupted and covered a city in hot ash.

Sesame panicked and out popped what she had been going to say to Maddy.

"Karisma!"

"No," said Mrs Wilks, giving Sesame a quizzical look. "I've never heard of *that* place. You must tell us about it sometime!"

The class giggled and Sesame wriggled in her seat.

"Anyone know the right answer?" said Mrs Wilks.

"Pompeii," said Olivia, who always paid attention.

Luckily for Sesame the bell went, and everyone hurried outside.

"Phew!" she said, as she and Maddy walked across the playground. "Supposing Mrs Wilks had made me talk about Karisma?"

"Well you've got to tell *me* about it," said Maddy. "You promised. Remember?"

It was true. Sesame had promised but, since then, she hadn't found the right time. And it couldn't be now because her gran, Lossy, and Mrs Webb were waiting to collect them from school.

"Tell you at sleepover tonight!" she said, giving Maddy their secret sign:

= True. I'll keep my word!

"Remember to bring your riding stuff for tomorrow," said Sesame. She knew how forgetful her friend could be.

"I will," said Maddy. "See you later!"

That evening, Maddy arrived at Sesame's house with a bulging bag. She had packed pyjamas, wash kit, food for a feast and all her riding gear. Unusually for Maddy, she hadn't forgotten a thing!

Mrs Webb and Sesame's dad chatted on the doorstep.

"Sorry, Nic," said Mrs Webb. "Looks like Maddy's come for a week not a night!"

Nic grinned.

"That's fine," he said, helping Maddy with her bag.

"They'll probably spend half the night gossiping," said Mrs Webb. "You know what they're like."

"I do!" said Nic. "Anyway, I'll drop them at the stables in the morning, on my way to work. That's if they're up in time."

"I heard that, Dad!" shouted Sesame, as she and Maddy struggled upstairs with the bag. "*We* will be ready way before *you*. So there!"

Their parents laughed.

"They probably will," said Nic. "Ready to ride at the crack of dawn!"

Sometimes Sesame and Maddy had sleepovers with their friends, Gemma and Liz. Those times were fun but tonight was extra special because it was just the two of them; actually four with the kittens, Chips and Pins, who'd crept up to Sesame's room to be with the girls. Sesame and Maddy loved spending time together. They would tell each other secrets they'd never tell anyone else. Although for Sesame there was her dad, and her gran Lossy. Ever since Sesame's mum had died, Lossy had been like a mother. But still, there were some things Sesame felt she couldn't talk about, even to her. Like going to Karisma! It was a secret she would share only with Maddy – for the time being.

Sesame picked up her teddy, Alfie, and held him tight.

"Remember that day I was waiting for you outside Tip Tops?" she began.

"Mmm," said Maddy, chewing a sweet. "I was late, as usual!"

Maddy sat spellbound as Sesame told her how she had fallen into a strange world called Karisma. How she had met and helped two tunganoras★ called Fig

* *

★ **Tunganora** – a small ape-like animal with long, pink shaggy hair, found only in Karisma. Their natural habitat is the Dark Forest, where they feed on the blue-spotted leaves of the tuntree

21

and Hob, who lived in the Dark Forest. How she had found a beautiful silver bracelet, with one heart charm, which belonged to Queen Charm. And finally, how Hob had helped her escape from a ghastly creature called a gribbler. By the end, Maddy's eyes and mouth were open wide in astonishment.

"Ses!" she whispered. "Did all that *really* happen? Honestly?"

"Yes," said Sesame. "Look."

She plonked Alfie on the pillow and picked up the jewellery box she always kept by her bed. First she showed Maddy the curious painting on the lid.

"Is it a code?" asked Maddy, examining the strange symbols.

"Yes," said Sesame, excitedly. "It took me ages but I cracked it. It spells 'CHARM BRACELET.'" Then she opened the box and revealed her biggest secret of all. There, on a tray, was Queen Charm's silver bracelet. And in a little section by itself, a heart charm with a tiny lock.

"Oh," gasped Maddy.

"The thing is, I've *got* to go back," said Sesame. "Twelve charms are still missing."

When Maddy looked more closely at the bracelet, she saw the empty rings where the other charms should be.

"I wonder what they are?" she said.

Sesame told her about the hedge she'd seen around Charm's palace gardens; it had shapes of all the charms clipped into it. She shut her eyes and tried to remember them.

"I saw a cat and a dolphin, a moon and star . . . a seashell, cloverleaf and . . . butterfly."

"That's seven," said Maddy, silently counting as Sesame spoke.

"Right," said Sesame, thinking hard. "I'm sure there was a horseshoe and a snowflake . . . a lantern and . . . a round one that could have been a coin. Oh, and a key!"

"That's twelve," said Maddy.

"And the heart makes thirteen!" said Sesame. "I've got to go back and find the missing ones. It's important Queen Charm has them back. Anyway, I want to know what happened to Hob. Supposing that gribbler . . ."

"How?" asked Maddy. "I mean, how will you get to Karisma?"

"That's the trouble," said Sesame. "I don't understand how I got there. So I haven't a clue how to get back!"

23

Three

"**W**e're losing silver!" said the Silversmith. Her words echoed eerily around the cave.

– S-I-L-V-E-R . . . L-O-S-I-N-G . . . S-I-L-V-E-R!

"Hushish!"*exclaimed the beautiful young woman standing next to her. It was Queen Charm. "First my charm bracelet and now this!"

It was alarming news to say the least. The Silver Pool of Mount Fortuna had always been full; no matter how much silver was used, the pool mysteriously refilled.

The two stooped to look more closely at the surface of the pool, shimmering way below.

"It's lower than when I last looked," said the Silversmith.

"Are you sure?" replied Charm, hoping against hope that she was mistaken.

"I'm certain of it," said the Silversmith. A frown wrinkled her delicate brow. "I noticed the change soon after your charm bracelet had been stolen. At

* *

*****Hushish** – a word used to express dismay

24

first I thought it was a coincidence but now . . . I'm not so sure. There may be a connection."

"What do you mean?" asked Charm, twisting a strand of fair hair round her finger. She was completely baffled; would she *ever* understand the Silversmith's quicksilver thoughts, flitting here and there, making pieces of the puzzle fall into place. "I seem to remember you thought Zorgan was involved?"

"Exactly!" said the Silversmith. "And something tells me he's behind this too—"

A sudden icy chill made her shiver and a ghastly vision flashed before her eyes. A dragon was writhing in the Silver Pool, fighting for its life! She gasped and shut her eyes. When she opened them again, the image had gone.

"What is it?" said Charm. "You look as if you've seen a ghost!"

"In a way . . . I think I have," said the Silversmith slowly. "Your Majesty, I believe Zorgan may have done something terrible."

"What?" said Charm.

"Well, he's probably furious because the charm bracelet won't work for him," said the Silversmith, her thoughts racing.

"Even if you're right," said Charm, "I still don't see how Zorgan can be blamed for this." She pointed to the pool.

The Silversmith hesitated before she replied. The full horror of what she was thinking made her head reel. When she spoke it was in a whisper.

"He may have put a spell on Agapogo to drain the pool. That . . . ghost I saw. It was—"

"Agapogo!" exclaimed Charm. "The dragon of the Silver Pool? But that's just a legend! A wonderful story, of course, and I loved reading it as a child but . . ."

She stopped. Something about the way the

Silversmith was looking at her made Charm realise she was perfectly serious.

"It *is* possible to summon the spirit of a dragon," said the Silversmith. "It's rarely done and no one but a magwort✳ would try it—"

There was a sharp intake of breath from Charm, as she took in the full meaning of what the Silversmith was saying. Instinctively, she went to clasp her charm bracelet for comfort. But of course it wasn't there.

"I feel so powerless without my bracelet," she told the Silversmith. "I need it now more than ever!"

Since her charm bracelet had been stolen, things had taken a turn for the worse. There had been a dramatic change in the weather – everyone was talking about it! Most of the summer crops had been ruined by heavy downpours of rain, which were unusual for

✳ **Magwort** – Probably the worst name you could call anyone! General term for a fool

27

this time of year. The River Two Moons had burst its banks and flooded the surrounding fields. And, as if that wasn't bad enough, some skreel✴ had escaped from Morbrecia's lake; local farmers had reported seeing them, feeding off the carcasses of drowned animals. And now this loss of silver! It was a terrible state of affairs. She had to get her charm bracelet back and put things right.

The Silversmith read her thoughts; she'd been going to tell the queen some good news about the bracelet to cheer her up anyway.

"There's been a . . . development," she said, choosing her words carefully. "You remember I told you about the Charmseeker, Sesame Brown?"

"Yes," said Charm.

* *

✴ **Skreel** – small flesh-eating fish

28

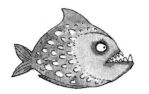

"Well, she found your . . . *bracelet*," she said, emphasising the word.

"That's amazing!" exclaimed Charm. "Where is it?"

The Silversmith took a deep breath.

"Sesame has taken it to a safe place in the Outworld," she explained. "She found your bracelet with . . . just one charm. The heart. The other twelve charms are missing."

Charm felt giddy with emotion. She was elated to hear her bracelet had been found, but devastated about the charms that had been lost.

"Is Sesame coming back?" she asked. "Will she help us look for the missing charms?"

"Oh, yes," said the Silversmith, with a reassuring smile. "Sesame Brown will be back!"

Four

Sesame and Maddy were up bright and early next morning, to go riding. They had finished their breakfast and washed up, long before Nic came into the kitchen.

"Come along, Dad," said Sesame, tapping her watch. "We don't want *you* to make us late!"

"Okay, okay, joke's on me!" said Nic, holding up his hands. "Be with you in five minutes."

He poured some coffee, grabbed a piece of toast and slung a camera over his shoulder. He worked as a photographer for *The Daily Times*. As Nic drove the girls to the stables, they chatted in the back of the car.

"I hope I ride Silver today," said Sesame. "He's my favourite."

"I like Muffin," said Maddy. "He's got a lovely soft nose."

"Sorry I can't stay to watch," said Nic. "I'm doing a charity fun run."

Sesame rolled her eyes.

"You're not actually *running*, Dad," she said, "just taking pictures."

"True," said Nic.

And they all laughed.

"It sounds cool anyway," said Maddy. "I'd like to be a photographer."

"I'm going to be a journalist like my mum," said Sesame. "We could be a news team, Maddy! I'd be an ace reporter, writing top stories. And you'd be taking all the pictures."

Miss Luck was busy organising riders and ponies for the first lesson. She had short, neatly cut hair and wore a smart riding jacket and jodhpurs.

"Hello!" she called to Sesame and Maddy, as they drove up. And because Nic hadn't met her before, he introduced himself.

"I'm Nic," he said. "Sesame's dad."

"Hi!" she said. "I'm Jodie. Jodie Luck."

They shook hands.

"Sorry I can't stay," said Nic, genuinely wishing he

could as he looked into Jodie Luck's soft blue eyes. "Work, you know," he muttered, feeling a bit embarrassed.

"Fine," said Jodie smiling. "Maybe another time? Sesame's doing really well."

"Yes," said Nic. "Definitely. Bye now, Ses. Bye, Maddy. Bye Miss . . ."

"Jodie," she said. "Call me Jodie."

Nic went off, leaving Jodie and the girls to walk across the yard.

"Please can I ride Silver today?" asked Sesame.

"Afraid not," said Jodie. "He's cast a shoe. The farrier is coming this morning. You can watch him shoe Silver if you like."

Sesame nodded enthusiastically.

"And me?" asked Maddy.

"Of course," said Jodie. "Now let's see which ponies you are riding."

There were six beginners in the lesson that morning. Sesame rode a chestnut pony called Fudge. Maddy was on Muffin. They walked, trotted and cantered round the indoor arena, while Jodie called out commands. Sesame and Maddy listened to every word she said.

At the end of the lesson, everyone untacked their ponies. Sesame and Maddy had just finished putting their saddles and bridles away, when Jodie popped her head round the tack-room door.

"Farrier's about to shoe Silver," she called.

They hurried across the yard to where the farrier's van was parked. It was like a forge on wheels. Inside were all the tools and things he needed. It even had a little furnace. Nearby an older girl was holding Silver. She was talking quietly to the pony, while he waited to be shod.

The farrier was busy heating a shoe in the furnace. He looked up when he saw Sesame and Maddy.

"Hello!" he said, taking the shoe out of the oven with a pair of pincers. It glowed red hot.

Sesame and Maddy looked horrified.

"Oh, poor Silver!" cried Sesame. "Won't that hurt?"

The farrier shook his head.

"Nope," he said, hammering the shoe into shape on the anvil. "This hoof's like your fingernails, see? Pony can't feel a thing."

"I hope he's right," whispered Maddy, half afraid to see what would happen.

She grabbed hold of Sesame and together they watched him place the hot shoe on Silver's foot. *Sssssssssh!* The horn sizzled and made a cloud of smoke. That was normal. But what happened next was not.

Sesame and Maddy stared at the smoke in a daze. They held each other tight as the cloud swirled around them. Only now it was more like a silvery mist. And, there in the middle, was a shiny horse-shoe, spinning round and round and round . . .

Sesame felt her feet leave the ground and was

aware that Maddy was still clinging to her, as they
fell into the mist. There was a sudden rush of wind
and then they were falling . . . spinning . . . turning
head-over-heels until,

Sesame and Maddy were up to their necks in water!

Five

The magnificent runghorn,* Stanza, was the first to see them arrive. As one of the twelve gatekeepers of Karisma, he had been standing guard keeping a sharp look out for Sesame Brown – a Charmseeker from the Outworld.** Queen Charm had told all her gatekeepers to expect Sesame at any time.

Stanza quivered with curiosity. He had been expecting one Outworlder, not two! And which one was Sesame Brown? He went and stood by the riverbank, waiting to find out . . .

"What the—" spluttered Maddy, floundering about in the water and frantically looking for Sesame.

"Make for the bank!" shouted Sesame, doing her best to swim there herself. Sesame and Maddy were still dressed in their riding clothes, which made swimming difficult. Sesame was

---

Runghorn – this remarkable beast has a magical horn, which can perform many useful functions

**Outworld* – the name Karismans call our world

making good progress, when she saw a small black fin slice through the water to her right.

"Watch out for skreel!" warned Stanza.

Maddy was dog-paddling nearby.

"What are—?" she began.

"Keep going!" said Sesame.

Eventually Sesame managed to crawl up a slippery bank; scrambling to her feet, she came face to face with Stanza. The shock of falling into the river was nothing compared to Sesame's overwhelming delight at being back in Karisma, where she was quite sure she was. There was a squelching sound as Maddy came clambering up the riverbank after her.

"Fairday!"* Stanza greeted them. He pointed his curly horn, first at Sesame and then at Maddy, and asked:

"Which one of you is Sesame Brown?"

* *

*Fairday – a typical Karisman friendly greeting

"Me!" said Sesame brightly, wringing water from her hair. "And this is my best friend, Maddy Webb."

"Are you *both* Charmseekers?" the gatekeeper enquired.

Sesame beamed at Maddy.

"Yes!" she said. "We've come to look for the missing charms."

Meanwhile Maddy stood there dripping wet and speechless. She couldn't believe her eyes. There was so much to take in, not least the fact she had suddenly and unexpectedly become a Charmseeker! Then Stanza introduced himself.

"I'm Stanza," he said. "Gatekeeper Two."

At last Maddy found her voice.

"Hi!" she said weakly.

"Sorry about the gate," said Stanza, casually waving a hoof at a nearby bush. "Not easy to find, I'm afraid."

Sesame and Maddy could make out a small wooden gate, overgrown with briars.

"No wonder we missed it," said Sesame.

"And we did get a bit wet . . ." said Maddy, water now streaming down her legs.

"Quisto!* Silly me," said Stanza. Straightaway he pointed his horn at the girls and they felt as though they were engulfed in a stream of warm air. In no time, their clothes were completely dry.

* *

✶ Quisto – an exclamation of surprise

"Thanks!" said Sesame and Maddy together.

Sesame had a quick look around at their surroundings; nothing looked familiar and much of the land had been flooded. Some fields were still underwater.

"Where are we?" she asked the gatekeeper.

"River Two Moons," replied Stanza. Then he pointed to a high craggy mountain nearby. "And that's Mount Fortuna where we have our famous Silver Pool!"

"What's that?" asked Sesame.

"Ah, you do not know the Legend of the Silver Pool?" said Stanza, wistfully.

"No," said Sesame and Maddy.

"Well," said Stanza, "I must tell you . . ."

Sesame was intrigued – always curious to find out about things – but she was keen to start looking for the charms. This was no time for a story! But Stanza had already begun and it would have been rude to leave, so the girls sat by the riverbank and listened.

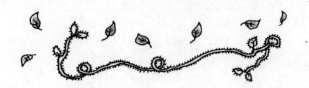

Stanza told the story well, recounting every detail about Agapogo and her vast hoard of silver.

"Poor dragon!" cried Sesame, when Stanza had finished. She was upset at the thought of *any* creature being hurt.

"Horrible," agreed Maddy.

"True," said Stanza. "It was a terrible way for Agapogo to die. But her legacy is the Silver Pool we have today. It has magical properties. The Silversmith used silver from that very pool to make Queen Charm's bracelet and charms . . ."

"Charms!" said Sesame, suddenly jumping to her feet. She wanted to ask Stanza about the Silversmith but knew they had to get going.

"Come on, Maddy," she said. "Let's start at the palace gardens.'

"Where you found the bracelet and heart?" asked Maddy.

"Yes," said Sesame. "The other charms might be there too. I left in such a hurry last time, I may have missed them."

Saying goodbye to Stanza, Sesame and Maddy set off at last.

"Gate Two closes at moonrise," he called. "Setfair!"✱

The girls were passing the bush where Stanza had shown them the gate, when they heard what sounded like the frantic fluttering of wings.

Maddy took a step nearer and looked. At first she couldn"t see anything, then – a sudden glint among the leaves. And she could have sworn she saw an eye, clear as crystal, staring at her. But when she looked again it had gone.

* *

✱ **Setfair** – goodbye and good luck

Six

Nix and Dina had flown like the wind from Zorgan's Tower. Soon they separated – two heartless pixies, each on a mission for their master . . .

I'm Dina. My mission is to stop Morbrecia finding the charms. I will not fail. Ha! Soon she won't be going anywhere, you'll see!

I found Morbrecia's castle, no problem. The princess lives near the Dark Forest, on an island in the middle of a skreel-infested lake.

Skreel are deadly dangerous but I'm not afraid of them! I skim the water and land on a rocky ledge below a wall. Then I scan the castle with my laser-sharp eyes. In seconds I know the location of every door and window.

I spot my target! There's Morbrecia in a room downstairs. She's screaming orders at a servant. Excellent! She is exactly where I want her. I look around. No one in sight. Good! Time to get to work.

I draw a vial of *Steely Crystals* cobweb-spray from my tunic and aim it at a window . . . Soon the spider princess will be trapped in my cobwebs of steel!

I'm Nix! My task is to track down the Outworlder, Sesame Brown. My master's memory spell tells me the troll in charge of Gate One knows a thing or two about her.

I'll go and see him first.

Ha! I took him completely by surprise.

43

He was having a nap, lazy thing! But he soon woke up when I twisted his beard.

"Tell me what Sesame looks like!" I demanded, twisting his beard tighter. And he described Sesame exactly.

Later, I came across some gribblers in the Dark Forest. A foul-smelling gribbler called Varg did all the talking - well, spitting more like! He told me about a couple of tunganoras who would know all about Sesame. So, I flew off in search of them.

I soon tracked down the ones I was looking for - a mother called Hob and her baby, Fig, living near Mount Fortuna. I hid behind a tree then ... I grabbed Fig and held him upside-down!

"Moomoo!" he squealed. I really frightened him. Ha ha!

Hob was afraid of what I might do to her baby. It didn't take her long to tell me everything she knew about Sesame.

By now I reckoned I had enough news to return and report to my master. But something happened that day to change my plans . . .

Flying over River Two Moons, I see two girls fall into the water. One of them is Sesame Brown! Quick as a flash, I hide in a bush and overhear the girls talking to the gatekeeper. Two Charmseekers! I can't believe my luck! I decide to follow the girls and tell Zorgan what they're up to. But as they pass my hiding place, disaster strikes! My wings get caught on a briar. I flap and struggle but it only makes matters worse.

At last I manage to tear myself free, but now my wings are torn and I've got to walk! I mustn't let them out of my sight. If I fail in my mission, I dread what my master will do! I must hurry to catch up with those Charmseekers . . .

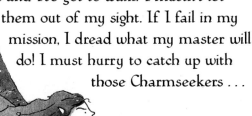

Seven

"There's a bridge,' said Sesame. "Let's cross and go into the Dark Forest. We can find our way to the palace from there."

Stepping from the light of the afternoon sun into the cool dark forest, the girls at once felt a sense of foreboding. It was strangely quiet among the trees, as they made their way along a narrow path. One side was flanked by the lower slopes of Mount Fortuna, where mossy boulders lay strewn about; on the other, wizened fir trees spread their slippery roots across the path. Sesame knew they were in a completely different part of the forest, from the last time she was there.

"I wish I'd asked Stanza for a map!" she told Maddy.

They hadn't been walking long when Sesame stopped dead in her tracks. A moment before, Maddy had been looking behind to investigate a rustle in the undergrowth and bumped straight into her.

"Ses! You might have . . ." she started to protest.

"Ssh! Listen," said Sesame.

"Singing!" said Maddy, surprised.

Out of the stillness the sound of singing floated through the trees.

"It's coming from over there," said Sesame. "Come on."

They fought their way through tangled roots, stopping every now and again to listen; the singing was definitely closer.

"There's something else," said Maddy, brushing a leafy twig from her face. "I'm sure I heard a horse neigh!"

"Me too," said Sesame. Then a few seconds later . . . "Look!"

A little way off, several riders on horseback were trotting along a wide track. Four uniformed guardsmen on shiny black horses surrounded a pure white horse, which was being ridden sidesaddle by a beautiful young woman. She wore a bright red riding jacket and skirt and in her long, flowing hair was a circlet of silver. They were all singing.

Sesame gasped.

"That must be Queen Charm," she whispered.

"Wow!" said Maddy.

And it was. Charm was on her way back to her palace from Mount Fortuna, following her visit to the Silver Pool with the Silversmith.

As Charm rode back through the forest, she had a lot on her mind. Only a few days ago she had visited some of the farmers whose crops had been ruined by floods. She had tried her best to comfort them but words didn't compensate for losing their valuable crops.

Everything was going wrong since the loss of her charm bracelet!

The thought of her bracelet reminded Charm of the song that had been sung at her coronation, when the Silversmith had first presented her with the magical charms. It had a lively tune and everyone knew the words, so she turned to her guardsmen and said:

"Come, let's sing the Song of Charms. It always makes me feel better!"

And they did.

Thirteen charms on a silver band,
United hold our world in hand.
May this gift for good Queen Charm,
Keep Karisma safe from harm.
One and all, beware the day
Charms and bracelet break away.
Together they must always stay!

Lantern, star and moon so bright,
Guide us through the darkest night.
Silver coin and lucky key,
Dolphin from the silvery sea,
Horseshoe, cat and clover too,
Fortune bring to me and you.
Nature's wonders please the eye;
Snowflake, shell and butterfly.
These precious charms should never part,
But be forever with the heart.

50

Sesame and Maddy were close enough to hear the words, as Charm and her escorts trotted by.

"It's all about the charms!" said Sesame, calling and waving with both hands, in the hope the queen might notice.

But Charm looked straight ahead and the cheerful singing drowned Sesame's shouts. Disappointed, the girls tumbled on to the grassy bridleway, now covered in fresh hoof prints.

"We can follow them to the palace!" said Maddy, as she watched the riders disappear round a bend. But before Sesame could reply, a shout came from a nearby tree:

"SESAME!"

Two tunganoras jumped down in front of her. It was Hob and Fig! Sesame was *so* pleased to see them,

she hugged them both at once. And when Maddy turned round, Sesame was lost in a mass of pink fur!

After Maddy had been introduced, it didn't take

Hob long to tell the girls all that had happened since she had last seen Sesame sprinting for the gate.

"I was so worried you'd get caught by that gribbler," said Sesame.

"I had him running round in circles!" said Hob. "He soon gave up."

Maddy cuddled Fig while they listened to Hob. When she came to the part about the pixie, Maddy looked up.

"I thought I saw something, as we were leaving Stanza!" she said. "An eye . . . something flapping . . . it might have been the pixie!"

Hob looked upset and began to cry.

"It's all my fault," she sobbed. "The pixie wanted to know all about you Sesame and I . . . I . . . told her everything I knew."

Sesame put her arm around Hob to comfort her.

"Don't worry," she said, "no wonder you were frightened with that horrid pixie threatening poor Fig. I'll deal with her, if I get the chance. You'll see!"

"Thank you," said Hob.

"But take care!"

Time was slipping by and Sesame was anxious to get to the palace and look for the charms. So, after many hugs and farewells, the girls hurried on their way.

And neither heard Nix, her footsteps light as snowflakes, following in their tracks . . .

Eight

Morbrecia's screams of rage rang through the forest. She was a prisoner in her own castle! Trapped like a fly in a cobweb.

Dina had been quick to carry out her work, covering every door and window, every crevice and cranny in a mesh of steel. One vial of *STEELY CRYSTALS* cobweb-spray had been enough to seal the whole castle!

Inside there was pandemonium, as Morbrecia ordered her servants to tear down the barricades. But all to no avail; the mesh stuck fast to the outside and no amount of pulling or pushing would shift it.

"This is Zorgan's work!" ranted Morbrecia, pacing up and down like a caged animal.

She stopped by a window and peered through the latticed screen. She could see Charm's palace, away in the distance.

"Or perhaps my dear little sister has discovered *I* stole her precious bracelet," she fumed. "This is all her doing! Or maybe . . ."

The last word trailed off as another possibility struck Morbrecia. She clenched her fists and stamped her foot.

"That Outworlder!" she hissed. "If Sesame Brown has been foolish enough to return. . . if *she's* responsible for this outrage – she'll be sorry! No one crosses me and gets away with it. Ever!"

For some time, Sesame and Maddy had been following the trail of hoof prints. Now they had reached the edge of the forest, where River Two Moons wound its way lazily towards a lake with a castle. The ground was marshy by the river and the track soon vanished. As the late afternoon sun slipped down through the trees, Sesame realised to her dismay there wasn't much time left and they hadn't even reached Charm's palace.

"It's getting late and we haven't found any charms!" she wailed.

"When do we have to be at the gate?" asked Maddy.

"Moonrise," said Sesame. "Whenever *that* is." She checked her watch and was delighted to see the dial had mysteriously changed, to show Karisma time. It had happened once before.

The girls paused briefly to see how it worked. And then came a piercing yell.

"What was that?" exclaimed Maddy.

"It came from the castle," said Sesame.

"Sounds like someone"s in trouble," said Maddy.

"Mmm," said Sesame, with a sigh of despair. She was torn between her mission to look for the charms, or helping someone in distress! But she decided they had to investigate. "Let's see if we can help," she said.

The girls squelched their way through the boggy marsh to a bridge, which was the only way across the lake. The castle loomed dark and forbidding before them, and they saw immediately that every door and window was covered in a fine steely mesh. Sesame and Maddy could see no way of getting in or out.

"What now?" said Maddy, as another high-pitched screech pierced the air.

They looked up and saw the shadowy figure of a woman, her hair flying behind her, at the top of a tower. It was Morbrecia. She had spotted them from the battlements. Sesame and Maddy waved, but Morbrecia returned their friendly gesture with a snarl.

"Balam★ Outworlders!" she bellowed. "Think you can defeat me, huh? Well, you're mistaken! I'll have you thrown in the lake. You'll be skreel meals in no time!"

"Oh, n-nice," said Sesame, trembling at Morbrecia's threatening tone.

* *

★ **Balam** – cursed, an angry exclamation

"Who is she?" whispered Maddy, cowering beside her. "What are we supposed to have done?"

Before Sesame could answer, the terrible whiff of rotting fish filled the air.

"Urrrrgh!" said Maddy, holding her nose.

"Oh no!" groaned Sesame, her stomach churning at the thought of what it could be. And when she turned around, she was confronted with her worst nightmare . . .

Standing on the far side of the bridge, blocking their way, stood a gang of gribblers – led by the biggest one, Varg.

Maddy screamed and clung to Sesame. Slowly Varg began to make his way towards them, dribbling slimy goo.

"Ssheshame Brown!" he sneered, drawing his thin, lizard lips over yellowing teeth. "At lasht!"

For a moment, Sesame and Maddy were rooted to the spot, frozen with fear. Then a blood-curdling yell from Morbrecia distracted Varg.

"Don't just stand there, magworts! Grab them! Move! Now! And get me out of here!"

After that, many things happened at once.

Sesame grabbed Maddy's hand and they leaped off the bridge, on to some rocks at the foot of the castle. The gribblers gave chase, lumbering over the bridge, grunting like pigs, while Morbrecia cursed them for being too slow. And Nix, who had been stealthily following Sesame and Maddy on foot, suddenly found herself trampled by gribblers!

"Ooof! Ow! Ouch!" she squealed. She stank of fish and was covered in slime. Nix knew she was beaten this time. She slunk away to return to Zorgan's Tower and face the wrath of her master.

Meanwhile Sesame and Maddy were nimbly leaping from one large rock to another, water lapping at their feet. Every so often they caught sight of a small, sharp fin, slicing the surface of the lake . . .

Rounding a corner of the castle they lost sight of the gribblers, now scrabbling about on the rocks; they were in danger of becoming a snack for the skreel. The girls stopped for a minute, to get their breath. And suddenly there it was.

"Oh, Maddy!" Sesame cried. "Look!"

There, glistening on a stone by her foot, was a tiny silver horseshoe.

"Ses!" yelled Maddy excitedly. "You found a charm!"

"*We!*" corrected Sesame, hastily stooping to pick it up. She held it in the palm of her hand – a perfect miniature horseshoe, with the tiniest holes for silver nails.

"And I'm going to have it!" said a cruel voice right behind them.

The girls wheeled round to face a pixie with flaming red hair and bright, crystal eyes. She stood there, threatening them with a vial of *Steely Crystals*. It was Dina.

"Hand over that charm!" she demanded.

60

"No way!" said Sesame, quickly recovering from her surprise at seeing the pixie. She clenched the horseshoe tightly in her fist. She felt fiercely protective of the newly-found charm, now strangely warm in her hand. This was why she'd come. Finding the horseshoe was meant to be!

"Give it to me," hissed Dina, "or—"

"—or what?" cut in Maddy.

"I'll spray you with this!" said Dina. "You saw what it did to the castle?"

They had. And they were in no doubt that Dina would take great pleasure in giving them the same treatment. Adding to their plight, they could hear the gribblers puffing and panting, getting closer by the minute. And the stench was simply dreadful.

"Let's swim for it!" Sesame whispered to Maddy,

quickly putting the horseshoe in her pocket. She refused to give it up!

But Dina heard her.

"You won't get far," she said. "The lake is full of skreel. They'll eat you in a grickle!"*

Sesame looked and saw the flash of a fin. She remembered Morbrecia's threat, too, and knew Dina was right. But it was their only way of escape. The two moons of Karisma were already in the sky; before long it would be moonrise. They had to risk it and fast!

Just then Maddy spotted some plants that, with the rising of the moons, were appearing on the surface of the lake. Giant moon-lilies were popping up everywhere, their huge lily pads floating on the water – like stepping stones . . .

* *

*Grickle – about the same time as a second in our world

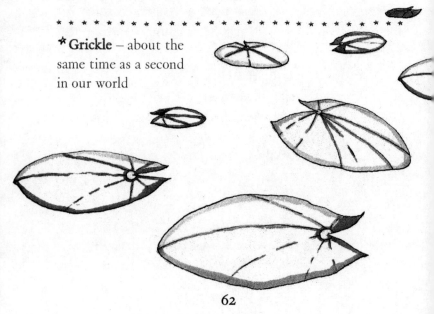

"RUN!" said Maddy, grabbing Sesame and pulling her over the rocks. "Run for your life!"

Thrown off guard, Dina lost her balance. She aimed a jet of *Steely Crystals* at the girls, but missed and caught two gribblers, binding them in a web of steel. And as Varg lumbered into sight, Dina flew off as fast as her wings could carry her.

The Charmseekers must cross Morbrecia's lake which is filled with flesh-eating skreel! Can you help them find a safe way across the water?

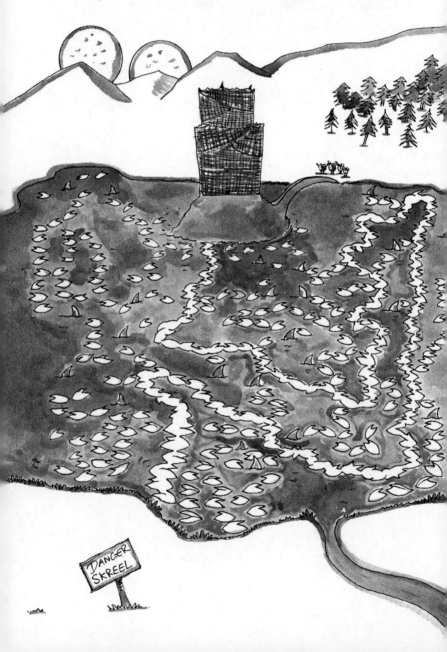

Nine

Maddy led the way, springing from one moon-lily pad to another, with Sesame close behind. Beneath them the water frothed and foamed; the razor-toothed skreel worked themselves into a feeding frenzy and leapt out to snap at their heels. But, at last, the girls jumped to safety. As they pelted away, the sound of Morbrecia's curses echoed across the lake; the gribblers were afraid of the skreel and had given up the chase. No words could describe her fury.

But now the enemy was Time! Sesame snatched a look at her watch. The two moons in the centre of

the dial were moving steadily into position, above
Mount Fortuna. When they were directly over the
peak, it would be moonrise.

Together the girls raced along a path by the river
– luckily, on the right side for the gate. They could
see Stanza waiting for them, and sparkling pin pricks
of light all around the bush.

"Run! Run!" Stanza shouted, his hoof pawing the
ground.

And as the two moons of Karisma settled over
the peak of the mountain – Sesame and Maddy
dived headfirst into the silvery mist and through the
gate . . .

"There, all done!" said the farrier, wiping his hands on his leather apron. Silver was standing proudly, displaying four new shoes.

"Good boy!" said Jodie, patting the pony's neck and giving him a titbit. "Sesame, could you lead Silver back to the stable for me? And Maddy, would you fill a hay net please?"

"Er . . .yeah," said Sesame, swaying.

"Hay . . . what?" said Maddy, dazed and confused.

Jodie looked concerned.

"You okay, girls?" she asked.

"Fine!" said Sesame, shaking her head and brushing silver sparkles from her eyelashes. "We're fine, aren't we, Maddy?"

Maddy nodded. She was still seeing stars.

"Mmm," she said.

"Here," said Jodie, picking up one of Silver's cast-off shoes and giving it to Sesame. "For luck!"

"Thanks!" said Sesame, with a beaming smile. "Come on, Silver!"

Later, upstairs in Sesame's room, the girls sat on her bed and talked about everything that had happened that day. The jewellery box lay open on Sesame's bedside table; inside were Queen Charm's bracelet and now there were two charms – the heart and the horseshoe – side by side.

"I still can't believe we've been there," said Maddy. "It all seems like a dream."

"But it's REAL!" said Sesame, her brown eyes wide with excitement. "And we went to Karisma together! We're a team, Maddy, like we said we would be, remember?"

"Yes!" said Maddy. "Best friends and . . ."

"Charmseekers!" said Sesame. "We're in this together now. It's our secret. You mustn't tell anyone. Not yet. Promise?"

Maddy nodded. "Promise," she said, crossing two fingers and pointing them down – their secret sign for *I'll keep my word*. Then she joked: "Anyway, no one would believe me, if I did!"

They laughed, but Sesame was suddenly serious. There were still eleven empty places on the tray in the jewellery box – each waiting to be filled with a missing charm. Maddy knew exactly what Sesame was thinking.

"Do you think you'll find them all, Ses?" she asked, quietly.

Sesame looked at Maddy with an expression of fierce determination.

"I've *got* to," she said, gently closing the lid of the box. "I'm a Charmseeker. I can't give up till I've found every one!"

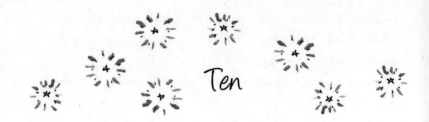

Ten

The Silversmith smiles to herself, as a candle flickers and dies. She knows another precious charm has been found, for it is the candle that bears its name that has just gone out. Ah, it is the little horseshoe! And now she "sees" it is safe with Sesame and together with the heart.

Eleven of the thirteen magic candles glow and each of them will burn brightly until its charm has been found – no matter how long it takes. And in time they *will* be found, of that she feels sure. Out of all the terrible things that have happened since the bracelet has been stolen, the Silversmith knows she can rely on Sesame Brown to do her best. There will come a day when all thirteen charms are united, returned to Queen Charm where they belong . . .

In the meantime, there's Zorgan and the Silver Pool to worry about! That stupid magician has gone too far. And for what purpose? To take his revenge on her for making the bracelet? To spite her because the bracelet wouldn't work for him?

Well, she has managed to save one precious cup of silver! An idea has been forming in her head – something perhaps she should have thought about moons ago! There is a chance she can resolve the situation and calm the spirit of Agapogo, which Zorgan has so cruelly used.

But that is another story. It must be told another day!

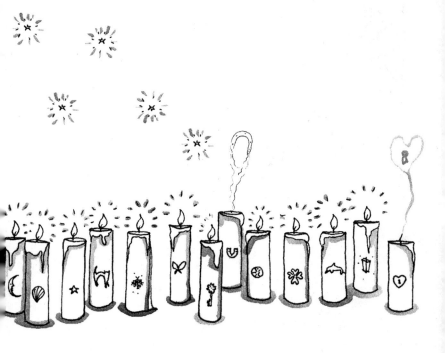

Acknowledgments

I owe a debt of gratitude to all those who have worked behind the scenes at Orion Children's Books and beyond to bring the *Charmseekers* books and their thirteen delightful charms to you. Since it would take more space than this edition allows to mention individuals by name, suffice it to say that I'm hugely grateful to my publishers and everyone involved with the publication of this series. In particular, my special thanks go to: my publisher, Fiona Kennedy, for her faith in believing I could write way beyond my own expectations. Her creative, tactful and skilful editing kept Sesame Brown on the right track and helped me to write a better story; my agent, Rosemary Sandberg; Jenny Glencross and Jane Hughes (Editorial); Alex Nicholas and Helen Speedy (Rights) Loulou Clark and Helen Ewing (Design); Clare Hennessy (Production); Jessica Killingley and Jo Dawson (Marketing); Pandora White (Orion Audio Books); Imogen Adams (Website designer – www.hammerinheels.com); Neil Pymer, the *real* Spinner Shindigs, for kind permission to use his name; and last, but by no means least, a million thanks go to my husband Tom for his inexhaustible patience, critical appraisal and support along the way.

Georgie Adams